Christina the Winter Wonderland Fairy

Join the Rainbow Magic Reading Challenge!

Read the story and collect your fairy points to climb the Reading Rainbow at the back of the book.

Special thanks to
Kristin Earhart

ORCHARD BOOKS

First published in the USA in 2017 by Scholastic Inc.
First published in Great Britain in 2017 by The Watts Publishing Group

1 3 5 7 9 10 8 6 4 2

A CIP catalogue record for this book is available from the British Library.

ISBN 978 1 40834 731 7

Printed and bound in Great Britain by CPI Group (UK) Ltd, Croydon, CR0 4YY

MIX
Paper from
responsible sources
FSC
www.fsc.org
FSC® C104740

The paper and board used in this book are made from wood from responsible sources

Orchard Books
An imprint of Hachette Children's Group
Part of The Watts Publishing Group Limited
Carmelite House, 50 Victoria Embankment, London EC4Y 0DZ

An Hachette UK Company
www.hachette.co.uk
www.hachettechildrens.co.uk

Christina the Winter Wonderland Fairy

by Daisy Meadows

ORCHARD

www.rainbowmagic.co.uk

Jack Frost's
Ice Castle
Sledging
Hill
owbound
odge
Ferry
Dock
ound Island

Jack Frost's Spell

Winter is my time of year.
Why should it bring others cheer?
Why do they like the wind and snow?
This is what I want to know.

They celebrate with candles and trees.
But winter should bring them to their knees!
Only I should enjoy the chill.
And so I'll break all others' will.

I stole Christina's magic things.
We'll see what havoc my crime brings.
No snow! No sun! No fun snow play.
Winter gloom is here to stay.

Contents

Story One:
The Snow Globe Search

Contents

The Frosty Ferry

"It was so nice of your mum to invite me on this trip," Rachel Walker said to her best friend, Kirsty Tate. She looked out at the blue waves churning around the ferry and took a deep breath.

11

"The trip was my mum's prize for winning a painting competition for her favourite travel website," Kirsty explained.

Mrs Tate's oil painting was beautiful – a stunning close-up of the details of a green pine-tree branch, dusted with crystal-white snow. The painting's background was of a serene landscape of snow-covered hills. "I've never been to Snowbound Island before, and this is the weekend of their famous Winter Wonder Festival," Kirsty added.

"I've never been to a winter resort, either, but the photos on the website looked almost exactly like your mum's painting," Rachel said.

"Maybe that's why she won!" Kirsty mused. "You know, my mum said she was

looking forward to
having a lie-in
and breakfast in
bed, but I'm just
excited about
the snow."

"I know. We
haven't had
any snow at
home at all," said
Rachel. Even though
it was well into December and almost
time to celebrate the winter holidays, the
weather had been dreary and rainy.

"My dad checked the forecast. He
said there would be tons of snow on the
island," Kirsty said.

"I think he was right," Rachel said,
pointing.

Kirsty turned to see a beautiful island.
It looked almost like a glacier, rising
right out of the crashing waves. From
this distance, they could see the ski slopes,
treeless paths that curved down the steep
mountainside. There was also a large
wooden building with smoke puffing out

of the chimney. Kirsty guessed it must be the lodge. As the ferry chugged closer, the water became choppier. Rachel lost her balance, and both girls laughed as they grabbed the railing.

"I can't wait!" Rachel admitted. "I don't know if I want to ski or skate first."

"Or snowshoe or sledge," Kirsty added, and then paused. "On second thought, sledging is my first choice. Definitely."

Just then, a door to the boat's cabin opened, and Mr Tate poked his head outside. "Brrrrr," he said as the wind gusted by. "The captain said the sea is too cold and unruly, so you two need to come inside. There are huge waves and chunks of ice. It's getting dangerous."

The girls glanced out at the ocean again. The jagged ice blocks seemed to have appeared out of nowhere, and they were floating right in the path to the island. The two girls took each other's hand and carefully headed towards the

door. They had been the only ones
on the boat's deck, but the cabin was
full of people in parkas, some carrying
hiking backpacks.

"Did you hear that?" Kirsty whispered
to her friend as soon as they entered the
calm of the cabin.

"What?" Rachel wondered. "I only
heard the wind and waves."

"I thought I heard some kind of bell,"
Kirsty explained. "Or maybe a chime.
Just as we came inside."

Rachel studied her friend's face.
"Really?" she asked hopefully.

"Really," Kirsty confirmed, a smile
twitching at the edge of her mouth.

"My fingers are crossed that you did,"
Rachel said, searching around for a
sparkle or some other sign. Chimes, bells
and sparkles gave both girls goose bumps
– and for good reason. Ever since the
girls first met each other on Rainspell
Island, they had been friends of the
fairies. They had met all kinds of fairies.
Each fairy had a special talent or interest
that was connected to her own special

magic. It was amazing how much the
fairies did in Fairyland and the human
world. Their magic inspired fun, beauty,
music, kindness and so much more.

It was also amazing how close
Kirsty and Rachel had become to
the fairies. The king and queen of
Fairyland now called on the two best
friends whenever they needed help.
Because pesky Jack Frost was always
drumming up new, evil plans, the fairies
needed help quite often. Of course,
Rachel and Kirsty were always happy to
aid their fairy friends!

"Do you think Jack Frost might be up
to something again?" Kirsty whispered to
her friend.

"I don't know," Rachel replied. "But I hope he doesn't ruin your mum's special weekend." She looked out of the window as the ferry tossed and turned toward the dock. "It's so pretty here. It seems especially evil for  Jack Frost and his naughty goblins to be messing around on the island. They shouldn't ruin everyone's chance to be in nature and enjoy the wonders of winter."

Kirsty giggled to herself.

"What?" Rachel asked.

"You sound like you could write for the travel website," Kirsty explained, but she knew what her best friend meant. A place like Snowbound Island was special, and they would do whatever they could to make sure that her parents – and all the guests – still had a marvellous time.

Freezing and Steaming

One of the workers from the lodge was
at the dock to meet them. She had on a
thick army-green coat with fake fur trim
on the hood and cuffs, and a thick
scarf covered her nose and mouth.

"Hi, I'm Devi," the woman said. It was hard for the girls to understand her through her chattering teeth, but her brown eyes were bright and kind. "Welcome to Snowbound Island. Let's go straight to the lodge." Without a smile or a nod, Devi rushed off with her hands in her pockets.

Rachel and the other guests had to hurry to keep up with Devi. Each step was a struggle. The snow was deep. Kirsty was surprised by the cold. The bitter air seemed to freeze her lungs, and it made her bones hurt. They were all relieved when they reached the lodge.

The lodge was beautiful. It had sturdy wooden pillars in the seating area and broad log beams in the ceiling. There was a fireplace in the centre that was made of large, oval stones, and a fire snapped and crackled. Best of all, the lodge was warm.

"I've never felt cold like that before," Rachel murmured to Kirsty, her lips tinged with blue. "It didn't seem normal."

Devi overheard her. "The cold isn't normal," the guide admitted. "And it is a surprise. The temperature dropped a few hours ago, and it's already a record low. The forecast says it will warm up, so we're hopeful that we can still enjoy many outdoor activities."

That was a relief! Kirsty and Rachel exchanged smiles. It would be horrible to have come all this way and not be able to go outside and play in the snow!

"However," Devi said, "for some strange reason, there isn't enough snow on the sledging hill. So the sledging hill is closed."

Kirsty's shoulders slumped.

"And so are the ski slopes."

Mr Tate's shoulders slumped.

Rachel looked out of the large picture window at the mountain above. From far away, it had looked like it was covered in snow. Now, she could see large muddy patches all down the slopes.

Next, she noticed a group of people dressed in tan and army green – like Devi.

They were all
huddled in a
corner of the
lodge, holding
clipboards and
shaking their
heads.

"Something's
going on," Rachel whispered to Kirsty.
"I don't think it's a coincidence that you
heard a bell on the boat."

"Remember Queen Titania's advice,"
Kirsty said. "We have to wait for the
magic to come to us."

One of the other guides rushed up to
Devi and mumbled in her ear.

"And there is no ice-skating today,"

Devi announced, trying to force a smile as she marked something on her clipboard. "Maybe tomorrow," she added hopefully, but her forehead was all wrinkled up.

"Um, there is magic happening all around us," Rachel said. "The bad kind of magic, the kind that Jack Frost uses."

Kirsty turned to her friend. It wasn't like Rachel to make such bold statements.

"We're only here for the weekend. I want to make sure you and your family have fun, so let's keep our eyes out," Rachel said with a kind smile. "I'll bet there's something we can do."

Kirsty nodded. She was on board. Whenever they helped the fairies with a mission, they always had fun!

"Time to go to your rooms," Devi announced. "We'll come round soon to tell you about the first activity." Then Devi began to hand out keys to all the guests who had arrived on the ferry.

"This one is for you," Mr Tate said, placing a snowflake keyring in Kirsty's hand. "We'll be right next door."

The girls unlocked their room and rushed inside. "It's perfect!" Rachel said. Cosy plaid blankets covered the beds, and the pillows had soft flannel covers. Rachel and Kirsty's cheeks immediately turned pink from the warmth in the room.

"It's almost too cosy in here," Kirsty said, taking off her coat.

Rachel quickly took off hers as well.

There was a knock at the door. "It's me," called Mr Tate. When Rachel opened it, he rushed in and headed straight for the heater by the window. He looked at the thermostat and turned the dial. Then he banged on the heating unit. "That's so weird," he said, wiping his sweaty forehead with his sleeve. "Ours is too hot, too. I'll go and tell the front desk."

"Thanks, Dad," Kirsty said as her dad left the room. After he was gone, the heating unit started to make banging sounds.

"That's odd," Kirsty said, leaning closer to the metal grate. The hot rush of air made her eyes water. She blinked back tears as she stared into the vent. "I'm going to turn this all the way off," Kirsty announced.

As soon as the dial hit OFF, there was another noise. But this time it sounded like the clang of a bell. Almost immediately, a fabulous fairy burst out

of the vent, flapping ice-blue wings that
shimmered in the afternoon light!

Wacky Winter Weather

"Thank goodness! I escaped!" the fairy
exclaimed. "That heater was scorching
hot!" She pulled a blue woolly hat from
her head and fanned her face. "It was
like an oven in there!" The little fairy
took a moment to catch her breath, and

the girls looked at her in awe.

She was wearing a lovely red coat with big buttons. Her thick, black, curly hair came down to her shoulders, and she was wearing shiny red ankle boots with a black bow on them.

As Kirsty and Rachel watched, the fairy pulled out her wand and whispered a charm. At once, a burst of tiny snow globes sprang from the wand and fell over her like a snow shower. The fairy sighed. "My wand has built-in air conditioning," she explained. "That's better." The fairy placed her wand between her teeth and held it there as she put her hat back on her head. Then she introduced herself. "My name is

Christina, and I am
the Winter Wonderland
Fairy," she said with a
smile. "As you might
guess, I love winter!"

"We love it, too," Kirsty
said to the fairy.

"I'm Rachel, and this
is Kirsty," Rachel said.
"We were wondering if we
might meet a fairy here on
the island!"

"Well, Snowbound Island
is always a magical place,"
Christina said. "But things are a bit
strange around here now. I'll bet you
can guess why. Jack Frost is up to his old

tricks. His goblins stole my three magical items – the ones that help me make winter wonderful for everyone in the human and the fairy worlds."

"Do you know where your items are?" Kirsty asked.

"Well, I suspect that they are somewhere on the island. When Jack Frost zapped my items into the human world, he sent me and a bunch of his goblins, too. I ended up stuck in this heating vent. It was horrible! I think you broke Jack Frost's spell when you turned the heat all the way off. Thank you," Christina said.

Kirsty felt herself blush. "I was happy to help. What else can we do?"

"I need to track down my three special objects. Will you help me?" As Christina asked, she closed her eyes and crossed her fingers. "Pretty please?"

"Of course we will," Rachel said. "What are we looking for?"

"My three objects are super cool, and not just because they protect the coolest season," Christina began to explain. "The first object is a snow globe. The snow globe makes sure there is enough snow for everyone to enjoy all the fun activities of winter." Christina then began to list all her

favourite snow activities, which took a long time. She obviously loved winter!

"The second object is a hat that looks a lot like the one I'm wearing." She pointed to her own woolly hat with her wand. "It has ears, too. It allows people to enjoy being outside, even though winter can get very chilly.

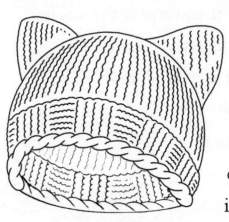

"Object number three is very special, even though its importance is hard to explain. It is a bright yellow candle that I keep in a snowflake lantern. The candle represents how the days are

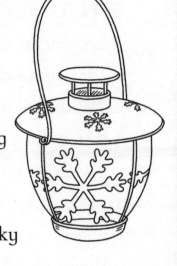

shorter during winter, but also how they begin to get longer again after the winter solstice," Christina said. "The solstice is coming soon. I hope we have the candle back by then, or some really weird and wacky things might happen."

"Like what?" Kirsty asked.

"I can't be sure, really," Christina said. "But we should keep a lookout for it all the time."

Just then, there was a knock at the door. "Quick, Christina, hide in my pocket!" Rachel instructed. The fairy did so, grumbling about how hot it was.

"Hello, girls," Devi said with a smile, when Kirsty opened the door. "It's time for a sleigh ride!"

"With real horses?" Rachel asked her hopefully.

"With real horses," Devi answered, nodding. "We'll be touring the island. There's lots to see!"

Kirsty and Rachel smiled at each other. That sounded like so much fun! The girls quickly gathered their warmest outdoor gear and hurried to the seating area in front of the lodge.

"Don't forget to put your scarf over your mouth," Mrs Tate said to both girls as they went outside. "And cover your ears," she added, adjusting Kirsty's hood.

"Don't worry, Mum. We'll be fine," Kirsty assured her.

"But it really is dreadfully cold," Mrs Tate said.

"Yes, but all the sleighs have heated seats. They are very fancy," Devi told them. "Let's head outside!"

All the guests taking part headed out together through the lodge's front doors.

Devi helped Mr and Mrs Tate into their sleigh seats. Kirsty and Rachel stroked the horses while they waited.

"This is going to be the best day ever," Kirsty said.

"There is one thing that would make it better," Rachel said, "and that's if it were snowing." Rachel felt a squirming in her pocket, and Christina peeked out.

"Find my snow globe, and you'll get all the snow you could wish for," she said.

"That's a deal," Rachel promised.

Sloshy Sleigh Ride

"It's so cold," Rachel said with a shiver. "I feel like my tongue could freeze."

"That's because my magic hat is missing," Christina reminded the girls. "It makes it very hard to be outside in such frigid weather, even though we're having fun."

The girls and
their new fairy
friend were
having fun.
They were on
a real sleigh
ride. Real horses
were pulling the
sleigh! The only
problem was that the
sleigh path was not very
snowy. The sleigh scraped over crusty ice
in some places. In others, it slowed down
and got stuck in sloshy mud puddles.

"I'm confused," Kirsty said. "How can
there be puddles when the weather is so
cold? It must be below freezing."

"Sometimes the ground is not as cold as the air," Christina explained, "so not all puddles freeze right away. But that's not what is happening now." Rachel and Kirsty looked over at her. "The puddles are because my magical snow globe is with the goblins. Believe it or not, the snow globe can do crazy things to winter weather if it is in the wrong hands."

"I believe you," said Kirsty. "Which of your objects should we try to track down first?"

"They are all important, so I think you should wait for the magic to come to you. Grab the first one you can find!" the fairy advised.

Christina's plan sounded like a good

one. The girls kept an eye out as the horses pulled the sleigh. The path they followed ran along the coast, and the view was incredible.

All at once, a grey, hazy cloud appeared over their heads. Then freezing rain began to fall. "And I thought I was cold before!" Rachel said, her teeth chattering. The rain was coming down so hard the girls could barely see, and there was a furious wind that whipped at the horses' tails.

Christina hid under Kirsty's hood, trying to work some magic on the dark cloud. "My wand doesn't seem to work in this rain," the fairy said. Her wings were wet and limp. "I'll bet my special snow globe is near. Remember, it can really mess up the winter weather if it's in the wrong hands."

Kirsty and Rachel squinted through the heavy

drizzle, but neither of them could make out a thing.

"Did you hear that whinny?" Rachel said a moment later. "It sounded like a happy horse, not a cold, soggy one." The horses pulling their sleigh were no longer joyfully trotting along. They were walking slowly, carefully picking each step along the uneven, icy path.

"Do you think there's another sleigh?" Kirsty asked. "Maybe one travelling on a smoother, less dangerous path?"

"Maybe a magical path?" Rachel added, suspecting that Jack Frost's goblins were not far off.

"There's only one way to find out!" Christina declared. She gave her wings a shake and raised her wand.

What we need is a sleigh-ride gift.
With less gravity we will get a lift.
No mucky puddles or rocky ice,
Our path will now be smooth and nice.
Horses, sleigh and passengers, too,
Will speed along for a better view.

Before the girls had time to think about the magic charm, it began to work. Christina had created a tiny sleigh pulled by two tiny horses! With another swish of her wand, she shrank them and transported them to the new, miniature sleigh.

51

Get That Globe!

The fairy-size sleigh zoomed above
the trees.

"What about my parents?" Kirsty
asked, pointing.

"Not to worry," Christina said, "I used
a special spell, so they won't notice. I
hope we won't be gone long."

Another series of happy whinnies rang through the air.

"Those other horses are close," Rachel called out. "How will we find them?"

"It won't take long," Christina announced with confidence.

The tiny horses seemed to love galloping up in the air. They sped ahead, rising and dipping along the tops of the ice-covered trees. They were small enough that they could dodge the freezing rain. But the ice was heavy. It made the limbs of the trees droop from the weight.

Before too long, the rain stopped and the wind calmed. It would have been fun if the girls weren't so worried about Christina's snow globe. "We must be

getting close," Christina said after a while. "The weather is lovely here."

"There's snow!" Kirsty cheered. A humungous snowflake floated by. It looked like a fancy piece of lace made of ice crystals.

"And there's the other sleigh!" Rachel called out, pointing down between the evergreens.

Sure enough,
there were two
goblins in
the seat of
the sleigh. One
was jerking the
horses' reins
back and forth.
The other had both hands in the air. He
was shaking something.

"He shouldn't shake my snow globe
like that!" Christina cried, concerned. "It
could cause a tornado. We are safe here,
so close to the globe. But the rest of the
island is in danger."

Kirsty thought of her parents on the
rough and windy path – and the steep

cliff down to the ocean. "We have to
get your globe now!"

Rachel
seemed deep
in thought.
"I think our
best chance
is if we stay

small and sneak up on them. What if
we make a trap for the globe?"

In no time, Christina used her magic
to make some stretchy rope. The girls
tied a velvet blanket under the sleigh,
like a pouch. "That should hold it,"
Rachel said, satisfied. Next, Christina
told the horses about their plan. Finally,
it was time to act.

The tiny horses raced forward, their mighty hooves beating through the frosty air. They quickly caught up to the other, much larger, sleigh. Christina flew up and landed on one horse's back. "Pull up to the goblin with his hands in the air!" Christina called out. "The one on the left." The horses nickered, agreeing. "Girls, are you ready?" added the fairy.

Both Rachel and Kirsty took a deep breath and gave a thumbs-up.

The horses galloped even faster. Soon, they were level with the other sleigh. They snorted and pulled up, so the tiny sleigh was right next to the goblin on the left.

"Now!" Rachel and Kirsty yelled

together, and they leaned out of the back of the sleigh. They both grabbed the snow globe and held on with all their might. The goblin didn't even notice them until it was too late.

"Wait! What? Stop!" the confused goblin yelled when the snow globe escaped his grasp. "Fairies! Noooooo!"

The girls dropped the heavy, oversize globe into the special velvet pouch that they had rigged up.

"Now!" Christina cried to the tiny horses. "Turn left now!"

At once, the horses darted away from the larger sleigh. They left the two goblins yelling and fighting with each other.

Christina flew off the horse's back and ducked under the velvet pouch. When she came back out, she held the magic snow globe. It had shrunk back to fairy size, but the smile on Christina's face was gigantic. She hugged the globe to her chest. "Thank you!" she said to Rachel and Kirsty. "Just watch; this is for you."

The fairy leaned
down and placed
a gentle kiss on
the dome of the
globe. Within the
blink of an eye,
the most gorgeous
snowflakes began to fall.

They were big and lush — perfect for
sledging, skiing and sleigh riding.

The heavy ice that had been on the
trees was now gone. Instead, there was
a light dusting of snow. They looked like
the trees in Mrs Tate's painting again.

"I need to get this snow globe back
to Fairyland quickly," Christina said.
"But first I'll return you to your sleigh."

Christina raised her wand, and a cloud
of glitter burst around her and the girls.
In a blink, they were back to their
original size, sitting behind Kirsty's
parents in the sleigh.

"The rest of your sleigh ride should be
as smooth as silk," Christina told them.
"Or maybe I should say 'as smooth as
magical snow'."

The girls giggled and Christina
raised her wand again. Suddenly, each
snowflake seemed to sparkle. "This will
be one sleigh ride you will never forget,"
she said to the girls with a smile. "And
don't forget to look out for my other
two objects!" Without another word, the
fairy was gone.

"I hope all of the activities on Snowbound Island are as memorable as this ride," Rachel said, snuggling under a blanket that the guides had just pulled out. "But it's still cold."

"And it seems early for the stars to be coming out," Kirsty added with a shiver as she looked up at the darkening sky.

"That's because we still have magic objects to find," Rachel realised. "I can't wait to see which magical item we stumble upon next!"

Story Two:
Hot on the Hat Trail

Contents

Bitter Bitterness

A hazy light came in the windows, telling the girls it was morning. It was time to wake up and enjoy Snowbound Island! But the girls didn't move.

"Chilly, chilly, chilly," Rachel mumbled from under many layers of quilts and blankets.

"I know," Kirsty agreed. "I'm cosy under these extra covers, but I feel like my nose and ears have frostbite."

"I kind of wish the heater was broken again," Rachel admitted, "so it would blast hot air everywhere."

"And so Christina could magically pop out and surprise us," Kirsty said. Their new fairy adventure had started with the broken heater, just the day before.

It was the girls' first full day at the Winter Wonder Festival, and they knew the resort would have lots of fun activities scheduled. Rachel and Kirsty were

excited to
be taking
part, but
they also
had plans
of their
own. They
needed to find

Christina's other two magical items!

Rachel and Kirsty had seen how
messy winter weather could get when
Christina's objects were missing. Still,
there was good news. They had already
tracked down the magical snow globe.
Now, there would be plenty of snow for
all the outside fun. The girls could go
snowshoeing or sledging, and Mr Tate

could go skiing.

However, Christina's hat and candle were still missing. Rachel and Kirsty knew they would have to get them back from Jack Frost's goblins soon. If they didn't, no one could really enjoy all the fun of the Winter Wonder Festival.

The girls got dressed as quickly as they could, teeth chattering the whole time. Then they rushed to the lodge restaurant. They found an enormous breakfast buffet there.

"Everything looks amazing," Rachel said, looking around hungrily.

"Yes, but I definitely don't want cereal or cold fruit. I need hot food!" Kirsty replied, heaping her plate. "Waffles,

pancakes and scrambled eggs."

"You should feel free to go outside," Devi said when she saw the girls. "But if you do go out, you have to promise me you will wrap up warm. It's terribly cold out there." Devi looked very serious.

"We promise," Rachel said.

Kirsty glanced out of the frosted

window. The trees were bent over in the wind. "It looks pretty bad. Maybe we should stay inside for a while." Then she dropped her voice to a whisper, so only

Rachel could hear. "We can let the magic come to us."

"There is a fun craft project this morning," Devi offered, pointing in the direction of some tables in a room off the lodge restaurant. Various craft materials were piled up in the middle of each table. "And there will be hot chocolate."

The girls smiled
at each other. Their
minds were made up!

After breakfast,
Rachel and Kirsty
joined the craft
session and began
making ornaments.

They listened to everyone passing by
while they worked. No one wanted to go
outside. They all wanted to sit by the fire.

Soon, Rachel and Kirsty wouldn't have
a choice. Before long, they would have to
brave the fierce wind and the brutal cold.
They had to get that magic hat!

For the Birds

"I like the idea of helping the animals," Rachel said. She was using three different kinds of seeds to make a snowflake design on her ornament. Even though she was enjoying the craft, she kept looking outside. It still looked incredibly cold.

"We'll put them on the trees for all the birds," Kirsty said. "Devi was saying that deep snowdrifts can make it hard for animals to find food."

"That makes sense. Many animals eat food from the ground," Rachel said. She looked around and noticed a group of

resort workers. They were gathered together and talking in hushed voices. They all looked worried. "Something is going on," Rachel said. "I'm going to figure out what it is."

Rachel picked up her mug and walked over to the hot chocolate stand. She stood as close as she could to the workers. She leaned towards them as she poured her drink.

"Not only that," a girl with thick raven-black hair said, "but none of the animals have their winter coats."

Lauren, who was in charge of the sleigh horses, shook her head. "The horses' hair is short and sleek, like it is in the middle of summer," she explained.

"It's like their fluffy, warm coats disappeared."

"I saw a bird that was literally shaking in its nest," a young man said quietly. His blue eyes were sad.

Rachel tried to hide her reaction. She didn't want the workers to know she had been listening. But the news was so tragic! She and Kirsty had to act quickly. Animals were in danger!

As soon as she returned to the table, Rachel told Kirsty what she had heard.

"That's terrible!" Kirsty agreed. "You think the missing hat is affecting the animals, too?"

"It sounds like it," Rachel said. "I hope the deer and squirrels and other wild creatures are OK."

"We can't wait to find out," Kirsty insisted. "We have to do something."

"But it's dangerously cold out there. Shouldn't we wait for the magic to come to us?" Rachel asked.

"I think it just did," Kirsty said, smiling. "Look at that window." Kirsty pointed. There was a message etched in the frost on the big picture window.

Join me, girls!

"It's Christina!" Rachel exclaimed. "Let's go!"

Luckily, the girls had finished their
projects and could quickly tidy up. Then
they rushed to their room to grab their
coats. "We need to tell my parents that
we're going outside," Kirsty said, tossing
her scarf over her shoulders.

The two friends found Kirsty's parents
in their room. Mrs Tate was sitting up in
bed, reading. She was wearing all of her
outdoor winter clothes, including her coat
and woolly hat. Her fuzzy mittens made
it hard to turn the pages of her book!

Mr Tate was busy waxing his skis. "Are
you going out?" he asked.

"We're going to hang our ornaments
on a tree! For the birds!" Rachel
answered excitedly. She held up her

ornament.
The pattern
looked lovely
as it spun
around.

"Are you
wearing your
thermals?"
Mrs Tate asked, her forehead wrinkled
with concern.

Kirsty nodded. "Two sets!"

"Don't forget your gloves," Mr Tate
added. "And come in before you're too
cold."

The girls promised to be careful and
then rushed to the lodge's lobby. Kirsty
zipped her coat up to her chin and then

pulled the heavy door open.

"I hope Christina's still here," Rachel
whispered.

"I certainly am," a tiny, silvery voice
declared.

But just as Rachel and Kirsty turned
towards Christina's voice, a gust of wind
nearly blew them over. They stumbled
back into the closed lodge door. The
wind pressed against them, and tiny
pieces of ice pricked their faces. The
cold air swept into their lungs. The cold
seemed to freeze them in place. They
couldn't even move!

A Charm Against the Chill

"I'm stuck," Kirsty mumbled through clenched teeth. "Frozen. Can't move."

"Oh no!" Christina cried. "This is the work of Jack Frost, no doubt. Let me see if I can help you." She twirled her wand in one hand. "I think I've got just the spell! It will help you, but won't affect the natural world," Christina said. The fairy took a deep breath, closed her eyes and raised her wand.

When snowdrifts are high
And temperatures low,
The winter's deep freeze
Causes nothing but woe.
The cold air still bites,
The snowflakes still flurry.
But remove the chill
From these girls in a hurry.

At once, Rachel could feel a warm glow inside her chest. It began to expand. As soon as she realised she could move again, she turned to look at Kirsty. Her best friend had a look of relief on her face.

"Phew!"
Christina
exclaimed.
"I'm so glad
that worked."
She glanced
around at
the trees,

the clouds and the snow on the ground.
"The spell doesn't seem to have affected
anything else, so that's good."

"That *is* a good thing," Rachel agreed.

"But it wouldn't be good if someone
saw you, Christina." Kirsty glanced at the
lodge. She hoped no one was watching.
"Why don't you hide in my hood?" she
suggested.

natural world," Christina said. The fairy
took a deep breath,
closed her eyes and
raised her wand.

*When snowdrifts are high
And temperatures low,
The winter's deep freeze
Causes nothing but woe.
The cold air still bites,
The snowflakes still
flurry.
But remove the chill
From these girls in a
hurry.*

At once, Rachel could feel a warm
glow inside her chest. It began to expand.

88

At once, the fairy flew over and landed on Kirsty's shoulder. She then ducked inside the soft hood of her coat.

"I can tell it's still super cold out here," Rachel said. "But I feel warm inside."

"That's how the spell is supposed to work," Christina explained. "You should still be able to feel winter's chill, but you'll stay
warm enough to be outside and get things done."

"Like track down some goblins," Kirsty said.

"And get back my hat," Christina added. "Then everyone can enjoy being out here. Just look how beautiful it is."

Each girl hung her ornament on a tree branch, and then they gazed around, taking in the wonder of winter. The sun had come out, and the snow gleamed in its golden light. Every tree branch was topped with a

bright crust of snow. The air was fresh and crisp. Still, they knew that it was horribly cold. They were lucky that they had the warmth of Christina's special spell.

"Did you hear that?" Rachel whispered. "I thought I heard a voice."

The three friends did not speak, so they could pick up on any sounds. Everything was quiet, until there was a high-pitched giggle.

"It's too cold for anyone to be out here playing," Kirsty said. "The only people who have gone outside were the staff, and that's because they had to work."

"Those aren't people laughing," Christina said. "That's the sound of goblins nearby! I bet they have my magic hat. That's why they can bear to be out in this cold."

"Well, they won't have your magic hat for long," Rachel said. "Let's get it back!"

Gleeful Goblins

It was hard to move quietly through the snow. The top layer crunched when the girls put their boots through it. The snow was also very thick in places. The girls grunted as they tried to pull their legs out of the deep holes.

The goblins' giggles were getting louder. "We must be close," Rachel whispered.

"Shhhh, you don't want them to hear you," Christina reminded the girls.

Kirsty could tell there was a clearing up ahead. "It sounds like the goblins are on the other side of those trees." The three friends gathered together and peeked through a gap between the branches.

There was a large crew of goblins playing wintry games. The goblins were wearing hats, gloves and scarves, but not boots or trousers, even in the bitter cold. Christina and the girls scanned the group. They could not see Christina's magic hat, but they knew it must be close by.

Jack Frost's helpers all seemed to be

having a great time. They were throwing snowballs, making snow angels and even building a snow fort!

The hat *had* to be on one of their green heads. There were hats of all styles and colours. Some were striped. Some had super-sized pom-poms on top. One was extremely furry.

Just then, several goblins crawled out of the snow fort. One of them was wearing the cutest hat Kirsty had ever seen. "There it is!" she declared.

"I'm all roasty toasty!" the goblin wearing Christina's hat declared. "This is the best hat ever!" Then the goblin began to dance a silly jig. He kicked up his feet, slinging clumps of snow through the air.

"Can I have the hat next?" one of the other goblins asked.

"All right," the dancing goblin replied. He took off Christina's hat and handed it to the other goblin. "Just don't go far. We need to stay close together, so we can all stay warm."

"Did I mention that my hat allows everyone to enjoy the wonders of winter?" Christina said with a little sigh. "I feel bad, but we have to take that hat back from him."

"But there are so many goblins around," Kirsty pointed out. "How will we get it back without being seen?"

"The goblins are getting along so well," Rachel said. "They aren't bickering like they usually do. Maybe we could reason with them."

Christina
shrugged her
shoulders,
her wings
fluttering
behind her.
"We could
give it a try."
With that, she flew
out into the clearing,
and the girls followed
close behind.

"Hello, fellow fans of winter," Christina
called out, her voice full of cheer. "Could
we talk to you for a moment?"

At once, the goblins' expressions
changed from smiles to frowns. "It's a silly

fairy!" a goblin with fuzzy mittens cried. "She's come to steal the hat!"

"I'm not silly," Christina said with a smile. Her eyes sparkled with kindness.

"Don't listen to her! She'll put a spell on you!" warned a goblin with a long stripy scarf.

"No," Christina said. "Really, I won't."

"She'll steal our special hat!" yelled the goblin who was wearing the magic hat.

"We won't be able to play outside!"

Christina was usually a very patient fairy, but she had heard enough. "I am not going to steal *your* hat," she said to the goblins, putting her hands on her hips. "I am going to get *my* hat back.

Help me, girls!"

"They're after us!" yelled another goblin as he headed for the ski slopes. "Run! Get on the chairlift. Now!"

Before Kirsty or Rachel could do anything to help Christina, the goblins scampered away.

Terrifying or Terrific?

The goblins ran down the path towards
the ski slopes. Christina and the girls
watched as they piled their green bodies
on to the chairlift. Five goblins crammed
themselves into just one seat!

Rachel and
Kirsty climbed
into the next
available
chair and pulled
down the safety
bar. "I can't
watch," Kirsty
said, looking
down.

"Are you afraid of heights?" Christina
asked.

"No, but I'm afraid a goblin is going
to fall," Kirsty admitted. "They aren't
following any of the ski lift rules."

"Don't worry," Christina said. "I can
catch them with my wand if they fall."

The chairlift carried them up the steep hillside. At the top, the goblins scrambled out and tumbled into one another. They turned into a huddle of sharp elbows and tight fists. "You fool!" one yelled. "They're right behind us!"

The girls leaped off the chairlift. Soon, they were hot on the trail of the goblins. "The one with your hat is at the front!" Rachel called to Christina.

They saw a big red shed on the other side of the hilltop. Next to the shed was a line of large inflatable rubber rings. Just below the rings there was a long, icy slope. In the blink of an eye, goblins threw themselves on to the rings. They started to zoom down the hill, arms and

legs sticking out in every direction! They were all yelling.

"Yikes!"

"Ouch!"

"Noooooo!"

"Get off me!"

The girls ran up to the one rubber ring that was still at the top of the hill.

"That looks steep!" Kirsty said as she looked down.

"That looks fun!" Rachel replied.

"It will be! Hop on!" Christina directed.

As soon as the girls were safely on the ring, side by side, Rachel pushed off.

Kirsty gulped. Her stomach felt like it was still at the top of the hill, but they were flying down the slope at top speed.

"Wheeeeee!" Rachel yelled. A nervous giggle escaped from Kirsty's mouth. Up

ahead, the goblins' rings were bumping
into one another as if they were in a giant,
snowy pinball machine.

"We're gaining on them!" Christina said.
They continued to pick up speed on the
slippery ice.

"Wait! There's a fork in the path," Kirsty
pointed out. Up ahead, a cluster of trees
grew right in the middle of the trail. "Which
way is the goblin with the hat going?"

The group of goblins on rings divided
between the two paths. Christina and the
girls strained to catch a glimpse of the
magic hat. "Hurry!" Christina said. "We
have to choose a path soon!"

"To the right!" Rachel shouted. "Go to
the right!"

Kirsty and Rachel leaned all their weight to one side of the ring, and it slowly began to veer right. "We're going to hit the trees!" Kirsty warned.

Christina raised her wand, and a stream of sparkles poured out and surrounded them. The ring whooshed to the right, barely missing a tree trunk.

"Thank you!" the girls said together.

This path was narrow. It zigzagged around tree trunks and under low branches. The girls leaned from one side to the other, trying to guide the ring along the fast track. They could barely catch their breath!

"Easy does it," Christina advised from her perch on Rachel's hat. The fairy's

wings whipped behind
her with the changing
wind.

"I can't see the goblins
any more," Rachel
said. "Where
are they?"

Just then, the
friends' ring
zipped out

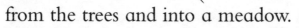

from the trees and into a meadow.
Up ahead was a gigantic snowdrift.
The mass of goblin rings was headed
straight for it!

"Watch out!" Rachel cried. "We're
going to crash into the goblins!"

As the tubes hit the drift, the goblins

slammed into the wall of snow. *Boom!*
Green hands, feet, and heads stuck out of
the frozen mound of white.

"*Brrrrrrr!*" the goblins all groaned. "It's
freezing!"

"Did you hear that?" Christina asked.
"They said they're cold. That means the
goblins don't have my hat any more!"

She lifted her wand and magically
brought the girls' ring to a stop. Rachel
and Kirsty jumped out and began sorting
through all the hats, scarves and gloves
that had fallen off when the goblins
hit the snowbank.

"I've got it!" Kirsty called out, and she
tossed the hat towards the fairy, who was
hovering in mid-air.

Christina twirled her wand, and a
cloud of sparkles swirled around the pink
hat. The magic item shrank to fairy size,
and Christina held it tightly. "Once I
take my magic hat back to Fairyland,
everyone will be able to enjoy the
outdoors again," Christina said. Then she
looked at the goblins. Some of them were

still stuck in the snow. Others
were shivering, their knees knocking
together in the cold. "At least
everyone is properly
dressed for the
cold weather,"
Christina
added with
a wink.

Without
another word,
Christina
vanished. The girls knew they would see
her soon. They still had one more magic
item to find!

Seeing the chilly goblins, Rachel and
Kirsty decided to give them a hand.

113

"I want to go back to Jack Frost's Ice Castle," the goblin with the fuzzy hat groaned as Kirsty pulled him from the drift.

"I know!" another goblin agreed as he snatched a glove from Rachel. "The Ice Castle is so much warmer! But Jack Frost won't be happy that we lost the magic hat." The goblins gathered together and stomped off, pouting.

Almost immediately, birds landed on nearby branches. The girls noticed squirrels trotting across the snow and a deer peeking out from the trees.

"It feels warmer already. The animals are coming out of their burrows again," Rachel said. "That's a good sign."

"I hope my parents venture out of their burrow soon, too," Kirsty said with a laugh. "That would be the best sign of all!"

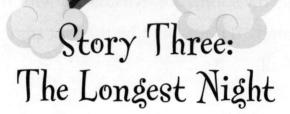

Story Three:
The Longest Night

Contents

It Started with a Spark!

Kirsty reached for the lamp on the wall above her bed. "It's so dark in here. I can't even find the switch on the lamp," she mumbled. She and Rachel had just woken up. It was the morning of their last full day on Snowbound Island.

"I'll open the curtains," Rachel offered.
She got out of bed and felt her way to
the window in the dark. She tugged
open the curtains, but no light came in.
"That's weird," she said, staring out. "I
wonder what time it is. It feels late in the
morning, but it looks like the middle of
the night."

"It's ten o'clock," Kirsty said, staring at her light-up watch. "So why is it pitch black outside?"

At that moment, Rachel and Kirsty both realised what was happening.

"This is all because of Jack Frost," Rachel said.

"Yes," Kirsty said. "We still have to find the magical candle, or the nights will just keep getting longer and longer, and we'll barely see any sun."

In the two days they had been on Snowbound Island, the girls had encountered all kinds of magic. Most importantly, they had made a new magical friend. Christina was the Winter Wonderland Fairy, and she was in charge

of making sure everyone could enjoy
the snowy season. Rachel and Kirsty
had already helped her locate two of her
missing magical items. Now they just
needed to track down one more, but they
might need a torch to do it!

"I know that the days are shorter and
the nights are longer in the winter,"
Kirsty said. "But why?"

"I'm not sure," Rachel answered. She
plopped down on her bed and pulled
the blankets around her. "But it's got
to have something to do with the sun,
right?"

As soon as Rachel said the word *sun*,
a tiny light appeared. It had a golden
glow, but it wasn't much larger than a

speck of dust. The light floated in mid-air, between the two girls' beds. It seemed to grow brighter, and it made a humming sound.

"It must be some kind of fairy magic!" Kirsty said. The little spark looped around

123

Kirsty's head, and then it swooped
past Rachel's. It seemed to skip its
way to the door.

"Quick! Put on your clothes!" Rachel
said. "We need to follow it."

The girls had never dressed so quickly.
"Don't forget extra layers," Kirsty said.

124

"With no sun, it will be extra cold."

When the girls opened the door, the spark flitted into the hallway. Even though it was daytime, the electric lights were still dim. Everything was quiet.

"It's like no one is awake," Rachel whispered. "Everyone must still be sleeping because there isn't any sun."

"But it's our last full day here!" Kirsty exclaimed. "I want my parents to have lots of fun. They can't just sleep all day! There's a snow hike and a campfire to celebrate the longest night."

The hum of the tiny light grew louder.

"Don't worry, Kirsty," Rachel reassured her friend. "We're both awake, and we're on the right track."

125

The girls followed the glowing,
humming spark all the way through
the lodge's silent lobby, out of the front
door and along a
snowy path. Not
until they were
safely hidden
behind a pine
tree did the
glowing spark
come to a
stop. In an
instant, the spark grew
even brighter and bigger, and it became
Christina, the Winter Wonderland Fairy!
She was still wearing her cosy winter
coat and her pink hat with the tiny ears.

"Thanks for following me, girls," their new friend said. "I'm sorry I couldn't appear as myself earlier. My power is very weak. Showing up as a spark takes less energy, so I can save it for real magic. That's important, because I have a feeling we're going to need it!"

Away We Go

"It's almost lunchtime, and it's still dark," Rachel said. "It seems so weird."

Kirsty and Rachel walked behind Christina. The fairy flew with her wand high in the air, so it would light their way.

"In some parts of the world," Christina

explained, "there
are only a couple
of hours of sunlight
in the winter. The
places that are
close to the
poles have
the shortest
winter days."

"Why is that?"
Kirsty asked.

"Well," Christina began, "as Earth
orbits the sun, it is tilted. One pole tilts
towards the sun and the other pole away
from the sun. The one that tilts towards
the sun gets more of its energy – its
light and heat – so it's summer there.

Meanwhile, it's winter in the one that is tilted away." The fairy paused to catch her breath. "Then, of course, six months later, the other pole is tilted towards the sun," Christina pointed out. "So they switch seasons."

Both girls nodded their heads.

"But that's science," Christina said. "What's happening now is magic. We have to fix the magic so

that science can do its job. Otherwise, everyone here will have winter and darkness for ever!"

"At least it isn't as cold as it was yesterday," Kirsty said, trying to look on the bright side.

"Yes, you were both amazing yesterday, and I have no doubt you'll track down my magical candle, too. It will be easy to find. It's in the prettiest snowflake lantern, and it's magic, so it is always lit."

The girls nodded again, and the three set off. They took the path down to where they had seen the goblins the day before, but this time there were no goblins playing in the snow. Next, they went to the barn. When they peeked through the

windows, they saw only the horses and
the sheep and the chickens. "Shouldn't the
barn be busy with workers? They need
to be getting ready for the big festival
tonight," said Rachel.

"I think people are still sleeping,"
Christina said. "Winter is a fun time to

stay inside and snuggle." The fairy closed
her eyes and smiled at the cosy thought.

"But it's a big, important day!" Kirsty
said. "If people don't wake up soon, they
won't have any fun!"

Rachel knew what Kirsty was thinking.
Kirsty was worried about her parents.
She wanted them to enjoy their time on
the island! After all, Kirsty's mum had
won the trip. Mrs Tate's amazing painting
of a winter scene had been awarded first

prize in a competition.

"I'll bet this is going to be the log for the big campfire tonight," Rachel said. She pointed to a large tree that the workers had cut in the forest. "But they still need to trim it down and get it to the fire ring. There's a lot to do!"

"This reminds me of one of King Oberon's favourite sayings," Christina began. "He always advises the young fairies. He tells us, 'You can only do what you can do.'"

Rachel and Kirsty looked at each other. King Oberon was married to Queen Titania. They were the kind, wise rulers of Fairyland. Sometimes, they spoke with grand words and

fancy phrases that sounded like
riddles, but both girls were certain
they understood what Christina had said.

"So, you're reminding us that we
shouldn't worry about what we can't do,"
Rachel said.

"But that we *need* to do what we *can*
do," Kirsty finished.

"Exactly," Christina said. "And we
need to find my beautiful candle in the
snowflake lantern. Once we do that,
everything will fall into place."

"But it's so dark," Kirsty mumbled. "It's
hard to believe there is light anywhere on
the island."

"Kirsty!" Rachel exclaimed. "You're
brilliant! The candle is not on the island

at all. I bet the goblins took it back to
Fairyland!"

A Frosty Fairyland

"You're absolutely right," Christina said
from her perch on Rachel's shoulder.
"If it's dark here, it must also be dark in
Fairyland. Jack Frost would want to keep
the lantern close, so he could have the
light in the Ice Castle."

Rachel and Kirsty thought this was good news, but Christina did not look happy. Her wings drooped behind her, and she was nervously biting her lip.

"Christina, what's wrong?" Kirsty asked.

The fairy sighed. "My magic is getting weaker," she said. "I don't have enough power to get you to Fairyland, and I'm worried. What if I can't beat Jack Frost and his goblins on my own?"

"Don't worry, Christina," Rachel said with a smile. "You won't get rid of us that easily. We have our magic powder from Queen Titania."

"We carry it in our lockets, so we can travel to Fairyland at any time," Kirsty added. "You won't have to face Jack Frost or the goblins alone."

Even in the gloomy shadows, the girls could see Christina's mood brighten. A smile spread across her face. "That's wonderful," the fairy said. "I'm ready whenever you are!"

The girls unzipped their winter coats. They dug under their warm scarves in search of their lockets. They had used the magic powder several times, but it always felt special ... and a little scary. Soon, both Rachel and Kirsty had found and opened their lockets.

"On the count of three," Rachel said. "One, two, three!" The girls took a pinch of powder and sprinkled it over

their heads. At once, the air filled with twinkling sparkles. Christina watched as a brisk wind wrapped around the two friends. In only a moment, the girls began to shrink to fairy size. The wind grew stronger and lifted them into the sky. Then – *poof!* – they were gone.

The three friends reappeared in Fairyland. Now, Rachel and Kirsty

had shimmery wings on their backs.
Something else was different, too. In
Fairyland, near the Ice Castle, there was
light. Even though the skies were filled
with a thick layer of grey clouds, there
was a warm glow all around.

"Oh, it's light!" Christina exclaimed.
"That must mean my magic candle and
lantern are nearby."

"We've got to track them down,"
Rachel said. "It looks like the light is
coming from over there."

"Yes, it's brighter on the other side of
the Ice Castle," Kirsty said.

"Let's go," Christina told the girls. "But
be careful. We don't want them to know
we're here."

The three fairies flapped their wings
and flew towards the light. As they
approached the Ice Castle, Christina
brought her finger to her lips. She wanted
to remind the girls to be quiet. Jack Frost
had goblin spies everywhere.

Rachel and Kirsty had been to the
Ice Castle before. The goblins often
stayed there, and you could hear them
squabbling ... or hear Jack Frost yelling.
Today, something special was happening.
Even from high up, it was clear that the
goblins weren't fighting. They were busy.
They had set up work stations and were
carrying supplies: wood, hammers, nails
and lights. They were building something!

"Look," Christina said. "They're heading into the forest. It looks like they're taking everything up that hill."

Christina and the girls followed the goblins into the woods. When they flew past, the local birds noticed them and chirped hello. "Shhhh," Christina whispered, hoping the birds would help keep their secret.

As they neared the top of the hill, there was a clearing. Here, the air was full of the sounds of sawing and hammering. The hilltop was also bright with the most beautiful light.

"My candle and lantern!" Christina said, pointing to a pedestal with the lantern resting on top. Inside the pretty

lantern with snowflake cutouts was a
thick yellow candle. Its flame had a
brilliant glow.

The pedestal was on a stage that the
goblins were building. "How will we get
to the candle without the goblins seeing?"
Rachel wondered. "They're everywhere."

"Yes, that's true. But we're such fast fliers, we can probably get to the lantern before they even know we're here," Christina said. Her eyes were full of hope, but Kirsty and Rachel exchanged a worried glance. They weren't so sure it would be that easy!

Snowballs and Snowbirds

The three fairies sat on a snowy tree
branch. They were about to set off to
claim the candle. Their plan was to
sweep in and out in secret, so the goblins
wouldn't even know they had taken
the candle from the top of the pedestal.

"We need to hurry," Christina said. "My magic is almost gone. I need the candle back as soon as possible. So let's go—"

But before they could take off, a small flock of sweet snowbirds perched next to them. The birds landed with a fierce beating of their wings, and then they chirped, high and fast.

"Shhh," Christina said gently to the birds. "We don't want the goblins to

know we're here." Without a pause she grabbed Rachel and Kirsty by the hands. "Come on, girls!"

The snowbirds chirped even louder when the fairies took off. Kirsty glanced back as they left, and she was almost certain that the birds were shaking their heads with concern.

Still, the fairies flew forwards, aiming for the candle at the top of the pedestal. Christina was in the lead. She sped like a dart towards her missing magical item. But when she was almost in reach of it, she slammed to a stop in mid-air and bounced backwards. *Whack*. The same happened to Rachel. And Kirsty. *Slam! Bam!*

151

"What was that?"
Rachel wondered,
shaking out her
wings. Kirsty rubbed
her sore head.

Christina reached
forwards and felt something. She placed
her hands flat and slid them along an
invisible wall. "It's a spell," she said. "It's
an anti-fairy force field. We can't get
to the pedestal." Christina's shoulders
instantly slumped. "What do we do
now?" she wondered. Then a giant
snowball smacked into her side.

"Fairies!" a goblin screeched.

"They're going to get the candle!"
another yelled.

"Snowball fight!" a third bellowed.

At once, snowballs came whizzing at the fairies. All they could do was dodge the sloppy balls of snow. But there were too many goblins and too many snowballs. Soon, the fairies were cold and soggy, their wings too wet to work.

"I can't keep flying," Kirsty called out.

"My wings are too cold." She could feel herself drifting downwards.

"Look! The silly fairies are falling!" a goblin called with excitement. "I'm going to catch one."

All three fairies tried to flap their wings harder, but they only moved more slowly.

"This one is mine!" another goblin called, pointing a crooked finger.

"Mine! Mine! I want to give it to Jack Frost!" A long-eared goblin jumped up and swiped at Rachel's snow boot.

In an instant, the small flock of snowbirds swooped in. Three of the birds carefully flew under the fairies and scooped them up. Rachel, Kirsty and Christina gratefully accepted their rides, holding on to the birds' soft neck feathers.

Three other birds flew up to the top of the pedestal and took hold of the lantern's handle. They weren't fairies, so they couldn't be stopped by the magical force field! They lifted the lantern, the candle still burning bright, high in the sky.

"Hit the candle! Knock out the flame!" one angry goblin demanded. "No one should have the light!" The goblins threw snowball after snowball, but none came close to the candle.

The red-beaked bird carrying
Christina knew just what to do. It flitted
up towards the lantern. "Oh, thank you!"
Christina cried.
The fairy reached
out. As soon as
she touched the
lantern, there was
a brilliant burst of
golden light and the
dark winter clouds cleared.

Safe on the backs of the snowbirds,
Kirsty and Rachel had an amazing
view of Fairyland from above. The snow
shimmered in the winter sunshine. Even
Jack Frost's Ice Castle glistened. King

Oberon and Queen Titania's palace shone like a crystal jewel.

"Thank you so much, sweet snowbirds!" Christina said. "I should have known you were trying to tell us something. You knew there was an awful spell around the pedestal, didn't you?" The birds all chirped in reply. "Well, Rachel, Kirsty and I thank you from the bottom of our hearts," Christina finished.

The snowbirds found a sturdy nest and set down the young fairies. Christina was anxious to return the candle to a safe place. "Thank you again, dear friends!" she called as the flock flew off. "And thank you, Kirsty and Rachel. It's time for me to get you back to Snowbound

Island and all the fun you can share there." With a flash of her wand, the girls were far from Fairyland.

Snow Globe Spell

When Kirsty and Rachel arrived back
on Snowbound Island, it was bright
again. As usual, no time had passed while
they were gone. It was nearly noon by
the time they walked back to the lodge,

and everyone was outside getting ready for the Solstice Celebration that night.

"I can't believe we slept until so late," one worker said to another. "There's so much to do."

"Can we help?" Rachel offered.

"No, but thank you," Devi replied. "You should enjoy this day. It may be the shortest of the year, but it looks like it might also be the prettiest."

Kirsty took a deep breath of the crisp air and felt the warmth of the golden sun on her face. The snow sparkled all around.

"This really is a winter wonderland," Rachel said, grinning.

"Let's go and find my parents. I don't want them to miss another second!" Kirsty said. She grabbed her friend's hand, and they began to run through the deep snow. They hadn't gone far when they heard their names.

"Kirsty! Rachel!"

They turned to see the Tates waving at them. They were standing near the lodge's equipment rental shed. "We picked out snowshoes!" Mr Tate called.

The girls rushed over. They were greeted with big hugs and a long list of plans for the afternoon.

"I can't imagine leaving without going ice-skating," Mrs Tate said.

"And I'd love to go sledgeging, too," Mr Tate added.

"Then, it sounds like there's something special tonight," Mrs Tate said, squeezing her daughter's hand.

"Mum, thanks for bringing Rachel and me along on this trip," Kirsty said. "It's been amazing."

"Well, it's not over yet!" Mr Tate smiled, fastening his snowshoe. "Let's get out there."

Rachel and Kirsty enjoyed a long afternoon of wintry fun and adventure! By the time evening came, they were more than ready to sit down and relax in front of the lodge's outdoor fire.

The big log the girls had seen earlier in the day blazed in rich shades of yellow, red and orange. The Tates and Rachel huddled together on benches around the fire. Rachel smiled and looked at her best friend. When something flickered in the corner of her eye, past a cluster of pine trees, she had to ask, "Did you see that?"

"I did," Kirsty said. "Do you think it was a sign – for us?"

The girls left the fire and followed the flickering glow.

"Pssst, over here!"

They weren't surprised to find that the voice belonged to Christina, who held her wand above her head like a searchlight. "Hello, Kirsty and Rachel,"

she said. "I wanted to thank you for all
of your help. Now, humans and fairies
can really enjoy the wonders of winter.
Just look at everyone!"

Kirsty and Rachel glanced back
towards the fire. Kirsty saw her parents
joyfully sipping hot chocolate together.
Some of the other guests were singing
songs together. Everyone looked really
happy and cosy.

"We should be thanking *you*," Rachel
said. "You've given us all kinds of
fabulous winter memories."

"That's what I'm here for!" Christina
said. "Also, I wanted to give you these."
She twirled her wand, and two rings
magically appeared, floating in a milky

cloud in mid-air. The
rings both had tiny
snow globes on the
with tiny silvery
snowflakes inside.

"Oh, they're
lovely," Kirsty said.
The girls each put o
a ring.

"There's enough magic for one special
snowfall, as a gift from me," Christina
said.

"Do you mean we can make it snow
with these rings?" Rachel asked.

"Yes, just twist off the top and shake
it, and then you'll have snow," Christina
explained.

"But it's so beautiful. I don't ever want to empty the snow," Kirsty said. "After this weekend, I think I want to trust nature with all the weather and the seasons."

"I agree," Rachel said. "And I'll also trust our fairy friends."

Christina looked very serious all of a sudden. "Your trust means a lot," the fairy said. "Thank you for being such amazing friends to the fairies. I'll look forward to seeing you again." She blew glittery kisses towards the girls and disappeared in a flurry of snowflakes.

Rachel and Kirsty pulled their mittens back on over their special snow globe rings. They linked arms and headed back

to the fire where everyone was having a merry time. "It's the longest night of the year," Kirsty whispered.

"Yes," Rachel replied, "and I'm glad I get to spend every bit of it with you."

Now that they had helped Christina find her magic candle and snowflake

lantern, things would return to normal.
The days would slowly get longer and
the nights shorter. After a while, with
more sunlight, the season would turn to
spring. Then flowers would start to bud,
and the snow would finally melt. But that
was months away. Rachel and Kirsty
still had lots of wonderful winter days
and cosy winter nights to share together
before then.

The End

Now it's time for Kirsty and
Rachel to help...

Samira the Superhero Fairy

Read on for a sneak peek...

"I love absolutely everything about
summer," said Kirsty Tate, who was
skipping down Tippington High Street
with her best friend Rachel Walker. "I
love the sunshine and the long days –
and most of all I love you staying with
me for a whole week. We're going to
have so much fun."

"I can't stop smiling," said Rachel. "I'm
so excited about this film."

The girls were on their way to

Tippington's little cinema. It was showing the brand-new summer blockbuster *Dragon Girl and Tigerella*, starring the girls' favourite superheroes.

"I can't wait to find out what adventures Dragon Girl and Tigerella are going to have," said Kirsty. "It's going to be amazing to see them in a film together – that's never happened before."

"What do you like best about them?" asked Rachel.

"I like the way Dragon Girl flies through the sky so fast when she's going to save someone," said Kirsty. "It reminds me of our fairy friends when they want to help human beings."

"I love seeing Tigerella use her

super strength," said Rachel. "Do you remember when she lifted a whole bus full of schoolchildren with just one hand? She's so cool."

"The best part is that they have normal lives too, just like us," said Kirsty. "It's only when danger strikes that they become superheroes. I wish I had a secret identity."

Rachel squeezed her best friend's hand.

"You do, in a way," she said. "After all, no one else knows that we are friends of Fairyland."

Just then, they heard a faint mew.

"That sounded like a cat," said Kirsty, looking around.

They were standing beside a high

garden fence with a cherry tree inside. As Kirsty looked at the tree, she saw a ball of black fluff clinging to one of the branches. A pair of scared eyes peered at her through the petals.

"It's a kitten," she said. "I think it's stuck. We should go and tell the people who live here."

The kitten gave another sad mew and Rachel tried to open the garden gate.

Read **Samira the Superhero Fairy** to find out what adventures are in store for Kirsty and Rachel!

Calling all parents, carers and teachers!
The Rainbow Magic fairies are here to help
your child enter the magical world of reading.
Whatever reading stage they are at, there's
a Rainbow Magic book for everyone!
Here is Lydia the Reading Fairy's guide to
supporting your child's journey at all levels.

Starting Out

Our Rainbow Magic Beginner Readers are perfect for first-time readers who are just beginning to develop reading skills and confidence. Approved by teachers, they contain a full range of educational levelling, as well as lively full-colour illustrations.

①

Developing Readers

Rainbow Magic Early Readers contain longer stories and wider vocabulary for building stamina and growing confidence. These are adaptations of our most popular Rainbow Magic stories, specially developed for younger readers in conjunction with an Early Years reading consultant, with full-colour illustrations.

②

Going Solo

The Rainbow Magic chapter books – a mixture of series and one-off specials – contain accessible writing to encourage your child to venture into reading independently. These highly collectible and much-loved magical stories inspire a love of reading to last a lifetime.

③

www.rainbowmagicbooks.co.uk

"Rainbow Magic got my daughter reading chapter books. Great sparkly covers, cute fairies and traditional stories full of magic that she found impossible to put down" - Mother of Edie (6 years)

"Florence LOVES the Rainbow Magic books. She really enjoys reading now" - Mother of Florence (6 years)

The Rainbow Magic
Reading Challenge

Well done, fairy friend – you have completed the book!
This book was worth 10 points.

See how far you have climbed on the
Reading Rainbow opposite.

The more books you read, the more points you will get,
and the closer you will be to becoming a Fairy Princess!

Do you want your own Reading Rainbow?
1. Cut out the coin below
2. Go to the Rainbow Magic website
3. Download and print out your poster
4. Add your coin and climb up the Reading Rainbow!

There's all this and lots more at
www.rainbowmagicbooks.co.uk

You'll find activities, competitions, stories, a special
newsletter and complete profiles of all the
Rainbow Magic fairies. Find a fairy with your name!